MARIE SPÉNALE

WONDER PONY™

BOOM! Studios, 5670 Wilshire Boulevard, Suite 400, Los Angeles, CA 90036-5679. Printed in China. First Printing.

ISBN: 978-1-68415-508-8, eISBN: 978-1-64144-666-2

TO MY
BOARDING SCHOOL FRIENDS!

BY

MARIE SPÉNALE

ENGLISH TRANSLATION BY

EDWARD GAUVIN

LETTERS BY

MIKE FIORENTINO

COVER BY

MARIE SPÉNALE

DESIGNER

JILLIAN CRAB

EDITOR

SOPHIE PHILIPS-ROBERTS

NOOO!
LOUISON, THAT'S ENOUGH!
DON'T LEAAAVE ME HERE!
I WANNA GO HOMEEEEEE! PLEEEEEEASE!
IT'LL BE GREAT! YOU'LL SEE! YOU'LL MAKE SO MANY NEW FRIENDS AT BOARDING SCHOOL!

OK, YOU WIN. WE CAN STAY A LITTLE LONGER.
WHY DON'T WE COME WITH YOU, AND SAY HELLO TO ALL YOUR NEW CLASSMATES?
WHAT A WONDERFUL IDEA! I CAN'T WAIT TO MEET ALL MY DARLING LITTLE GIRL'S BRAND NEW PALS!
I'LL SEE ABOUT GETTING A COT SO WE CAN SLEEP OVER FOR THE FIRST NIGHT!
URK...NO. THANKS, BUT MOM'S RIGHT. I, UH--I GOTTA GROW UP SOMETIME!
YOU SURE?
YUP.
I PUT A PACK OF BANANA CANDIES IN YOUR BAG!
CALL US, OK?
GOOD LUCK!

?
PSST
ARE YOU NEW? THE DORMS ARE UPSTAIRS.
HURRY UP. YOU'RE LATE!
CDI
UH--OK, THANKS!
LOUISON, RIGHT? HEAD OVER TO ROOM 5. THEY STILL HAVE AN OPEN BED.
THE LAST ONE.
5

WOOHOO! OUR THIRD ROOMMATE'S FINALLY HERE!
I'M ANN, AND THAT'S SAMIRA.
SAM.
NAME'S SAM.
I'M SO HAPPY MY PARENTS AGREED TO SEND ME TO BOARDING SCHOOL! IT'S MY DREAM! WE'RE GONNA HAVE SO MUCH FUN!
ARE YOU AS EXCITED AS I AM?
IMAGINE! A WHOLE YEAR WITH YOUR BESTIES!
UH... SURE.
I MEAN... KINDA.
UGH, NOT ME. MY PARENTS ONLY SENT ME HERE SO I'D MAKE FRIENDS, BUT IT'S SUCH A BUMMER.
I'M FINE ON MY OWN.

DON'T SAY THAT! YOU'LL LOVE IT HERE. YOU'LL SEE!
SURE, THERE'LL BE HARD TIMES, BUT WE'LL STICK TOGETHER!
AND THE GOOD TIMES WILL BE THREE TIMES BETTER! 'CAUSE WE'LL BE TOGETHER!
THE BEST YEARS OF OUR LIVES ARE WAITING! AND WE'LL SPEND THEM...TOGETHER!
LET'S START BY DECORATING OUR ROOM!
TOGETHER!

WAIT, HANG ON, SAM! I'M NOT SURE PAINTING THE WALLS BLACK IS THE BEST IDEA...
SHUT UP AND TAKE DOWN YOUR POSTERS, OR I'LL PAINT THE BATHROOM, TOO.
Dad? Mom? Please, I'm begging you, come get me NOW!
Please!
HURRY T_T

LOUISON
UH...HI?
OM NOM!
I'M NOT A SCAREDY-CAT, I JUST DON'T LIKE SCARY THINGS.
DAD GAVE ME THESE TO MAKE FRIENDS WITH, BUT I THINK I'LL SAVE 'EM FOR MYSELF.
GUESS MY FAVORITE FRUIT!
BANANA

WELCOME TO SIXTH GRADE. I'M MRS. RAMIREZ.
Welcome!
LET'S START WITH ROLL CALL.
ADA?
CAMILLE?
GAIL?
MAXIMILIAN?
SAMIRA?
LOUISON?
LOUISON?
AAH! WHA-HUH? HERE!
Max + Louison
DOES THIS MEAN WE'RE FRIENDS?

DRIIIING
OR... MAYBE NOT.
YOU OK?
OH! YEAH.
BUT I DON'T KNOW ANYONE, SO...
DON'T SWEAT IT. EVERYONE'S SCARED THE FIRST DAY. MAKING FRIENDS CAN BE HARD.
YOU JUST HAVE TO BE BRAVE AND GO UP AND TALK TO SOMEONE.
HERE'S A LITTLE WELCOME GIFT!
HEY! SPLITSIES?!
MAX CHOC

YOU HAVE A CHOCOTUBE, AND YOUR BEST FRIEND DOESN'T EVEN GET SOME?
OH, SURE! HERE!
THAT GIRL OVER THERE GAVE IT TO ME.
CHARLIE? THE FRESH-MAN?
I HEAR SHE'S THE MOST POPULAR GIRL IN SCHOOL. EVERYONE LOVES HER.
SHE KINDA FLAUNTS IT, DOESN'T SHE?
HEY, LOUISON! SAM!
OUR CLASS IS PRETTY COOL, HUH?
UM, LOUISON, WHAT DID CHARLIE SAY TO YOU?
'CAUSE SOME OF THE OLDER KIDS ARE SAYING THE SCHOOL'S HAUNTED BY THE GHOSTS OF STUDENTS WHO DIED IN THEIR ROOMS.
HAUNTED?!
I THINK THEY'RE JUST TRYING TO FREAK US OUT...

...THEY ALSO SAID THERE ARE MONSTERS IN THE DORM'S DROP CEILINGS.
WOW. DO THEY THINK WE'RE TOTAL SUCKERS, OR WHAT?
HA HA! YEAH! LIKE SOME FARTY OLD FAIRY TALES ARE GONNA SCARE US!
HA HA! RIGHT!
...
LET'S WAIT FOR EACH OTHER AFTER CLASS BEFORE GOING BACK TO OUR ROOM, OK?
OK!
TSS, TSS, TSS...
16:50

SEE ANYTHING?
NOPE. COAST IS CLEAR OF MONSTERS.
WHAT ARE YOU DOING?
SERIOUSLY??
BUT THERE IS A HUGE BOX!
HEY, QUIT MOVING! I'M TRYING TO--
OUARG
AAAAAAUHH

WELL, THIS DOESN'T LOOK ESPECIALLY EVIL.
DIBS ON THE CANDY!
I CALL NAIL POLISH! HERE, LOUISON. HAVE A PONY.
NAILS
TRADE YOU?
YOU SURE? THESE CANDIES MIGHT BE CURSED!
SWALLOW 'EM, AND THEY SPROUT TINY LEGS AND START CRAWLING AROUND, EATING YOU UP FROM INSIDE!
ACTUALLY, SURE. HAVE 'EM. I DON'T CARE.
QUIT MESSING WITH MY HEAD!
I THINK I'M JUST GONNA KEEP MY SWEET LITTLE PONY, AFTER ALL.

HEY! WE DON'T HAVE HOMEWORK YET, SO LET'S ABOUT EXPLORING THE DORMS!
WHAT FOR?
TO MEET THE OTHER STUDENTS? SEE THE PLACE? I HEAR THERE'S A LOUNGE WITH A TV SOMEWHERE.
I DON'T FEEL LIKE COZYING UP TO A BUNCH OF CREEPS.
BESIDES, TV'S A DRAG. IT'S JUST BRAINWASHING TO MAKE US ALL BETTER CONSUMERS.
OK! SEE YA! BYE!
C'MON, LOUISON! LET'S GO!
SIGH...
WHOA...*THAT'S* THE TV ROOM?

AWESOME, RIGHT?
EEEEE! LOOK WHAT I FOUND!
WE'RE GONNA THROW OUR FIRST BIG BLOWOUT TONIGHT!
KIM, TRY TO BRIGHTEN THIS PLACE UP!
ANAIS, NOELLE-- YOU'RE ON BALLOONS!
I'LL GO GRAB SOME SNACKS FROM THE KITCHEN!
THIS IS GONNA BE SUCH A BANGER!
NO, I DON'T THINK SO.

OK, KIDDOS: UPDATE ON SCHOOL RULES.
BY 9 PM, YOU'RE ALL IN BED. I DON'T WANT TO SEE ANY FACES PEEKING OUT OF DOORS.
AND PARTIES IN THE LOUNGE? FORGET IT.
HEY, WHAT'S THE WI-FI PASSWORD?
YEAH! 'THERE'S NO SIGNAL HERE AT ALL. I CAN'T EVEN TEXT!
YOU DON'T NEED TO TEXT TO STUDY.
HAVE SOMETHING TO TELL YOUR PARENTS? TELL US, AND WE'LL PASS IT ON.
WHY ARE YOU ALL STILL HERE? YOU'VE GOT FIFTEEN MINUTES TO BRUSH YOUR TEETH AND PUT ON YOUR PJS. HOP TO IT! AFTER THAT, IT'S LIGHTS OUT!
MOVE!
YES, NINA.

PSST.
PSST! LOUISON!
YOU SCARED OF LI'L PONIES, OR WHAT?
QUIT SHAKING, AND SNEAK ME TO THE BATHROOM, OK?
U-UH...OK!
WC
I'LL, UH...JUST SHUT THE DOOR, AND YOU TELL ME WHEN YOU'RE DONE.
NO, YOU GOOF, THAT'S NOT WHY I BROUGHT YOU HERE!
WE HAVE TO TALK. TOUCH MY HAUNCH THREE TIMES.
AUGH, YOU MEAN YOUR... *BUTT?!*

ZOUIP
ZOUIP
ZOUIP
LOUISON!
I AM THE SPIRIT OF THIS BOARDING SCHOOL, AND YOU WERE CHOSEN TO BE ITS GUARDIAN!
I WILL TURN YOU INTO **WONDER PONY** AS OFTEN AS NEEDED, AND YOU WILL FIGHT TO SAVE THE SCHOOL.

YOU WILL HAVE THE STRENGTH OF A PONY!
OF A *PONY?!*
HEY! WE'RE MORE JACKED THAN YOU THINK!
YOUR MISSION: TO RID US OF THE MONSTERS INFESTING THE SCHOOL!
WE'RE COUNTING ON YOU, LOUISON.
C-CAN I TAKE A HARD PASS?
NO EXCHANGES, NO REFUNDS.
POUF
I REALLY SHOULD'VE GONE FOR THAT CANDY.
TUT TUT TUT!

ANN
ALWAYS IN A GOOD MOOD!
I'M THE OFFICIAL CLASS PHOTOGRAPHER!
THEY'RE STICKY, SO I CAN PUT 'EM UP ANYWHERE!
PHOTOS
MY LED FLASHLIGHT, FOR TAKING PHOTOS AT NIGHT!
MAX STAR 2
LOUISON ASKED FOR THIS PIC IN SECRET.
I LOVE GOSSIP.

FRANÇAIS

DAY BROKE ON OUR BRAVE AND BEAUTIFUL SUPERHEROINE...
...ALONE--SO ALONE! AS SHE FACED HER EXTRAORDINARY DESTINY.
HER LIFE HAD JUST TURNED UPSIDE DOWN, AND SHE KNEW IT.
THE FATE OF THE WORLD RESTED ON HER SHOULDERS, AND NOTHING COULD CHANGE THAT. NO ONE WOULD UNDER--
HEY! YOU COULD'VE WAITED FOR ME!
NO WAY! YOU GOT COCO-HONEY PUFFS? NEXT TIME, I'M GETTING UP EARLY, TOO!
WHAT ARE YOU MOPING ABOUT?
I'M NOT MOPING! MY DESPAIR GOES MUCH DEEPER. YOU WOULDN'T UNDERSTAND.
UH-HUH.
WHAT ARE YOU DOING?
WHAT'S IT LOOK LIKE? DRAWING.
WHAT'S THAT?
A SLICE OF HAM?
WITH PARSLEY?
OR MAYBE...AN ELEPHANT?
NO?
SAM DECIDED TO TAKE THE HIGH ROAD AND LEAVE THESE PHILISTINES BEHIND.
A TENNIS RACKET?
THEY WEREN'T READY FOR HER ART. FOR HER.

NINA FLIPPED OUT ON US LAST NIGHT!
SHE'S STRICT, BUT IT'S FOR OUR OWN GOOD.
IF IT'S ALWAYS LIKE THIS, WE'RE NEVER GONNA HAVE ANY FUN.
WE CAN'T LET HER DO THIS.
OF COURSE NOT. DON'T WORRY
WE'LL STILL HAVE PARTIES!
IN THE BASE-MENT, MAYBE!
WE'LL NEVER GIVE INTO THIS TYRANNY!
WE'LL BAND TOGETHER! WE'LL ORGANIZE!
ORGANIZE WHAT?
UH...A RAD STUDY GROUP!
HMM.
OK, RUGRATS. ANYONE SEEN THE LITTLE BLOND BOY FROM YOUR CLASS?
IT'S NOT VERY PROFESSIONAL TO CALL US THAT.

HE VANISHED DURING THE NIGHT. IF WE CAN'T FIND HIM SOON, WE'LL HAVE TO CALL HIS FAMILY.
HOLD ON A SEC! YOU MEAN YOU HAVEN'T DONE THAT ALREADY?
PSST! LOUISON!
THIS IS A JOB FOR WONDER PONY!
LET'S GO!
SO, DOES THAT MEAN...NO CLASS?
NOPE.
WC
WHERE'RE WE GOING?
THE KITCHENS!

HURRY, WONDER PONY! SAVE HIM!
UH... OK.
UH...HEY. SHOO!
THAT'S ENOUGH! LEAVE HIM ALONE NOW!
WHAT THE HECK ARE YOU DOING?
THE STRENGTH OF A PONY, REMEMBER?
HAVEN'T YOU EVER TRIED USING YOUR WORDS FIRST?!
SLURP

AAAH
AAAH
AAAH
PAF
I'LL TAKE CARE OF THIS.
YOU--WATCH AND LEARN. TAKE NOTES FOR NEXT TIME!
YUP!

GNAP
SCRAA
CHOMP CHOMP CHOMP
SHRAM
HAH! NOT SO SCARY NOW, ARE YOU, MISTER GIANT BROCCOLI!
DID YOU REALLY THINK YOU COULD FRIGHTEN ME, THE INCREDIBLE WONDER PONY?
chomp chomp

SNAP
HUH?
AAAH!
I THINK WE'RE GOOD NOW. YOU CAN STOP.
ANYWAY, AFTERWARDS THEY ALWAYS...
...DISAPPEAR.
POUF!
EEW.
NOT COMPLETELY...
WOW! THAT WAS AMAZING!
Y-YOU'RE SO STRONG!
OH, IT'S NOTHING, REALLY.
JUST DOING MY JOB AS WONDER PONY!
GET TO CLASS, KID.
YES, MA'AM.
PINCH ME...

THANKS SO MUCH!
PRETTY GOOD WORK THERE, WONDER PONY...
...BUT NEXT TIME, YOU'RE ON YOUR OWN, GOT IT?
YEAH, YEAH.
SO...TURN ME BACK?
I'LL BE LATE FOR CLASS!
EH...I THINK I'LL RUN BACK TO MY ROOM FOR A NEW OUTFIT.

SAM
THAT'S ME.
I ADMIT I CAN BE A BIT DARK.
AT 5, I'D ALREADY STOPPED BEING CUTE.
I'M CLEARLY THE ARTISTE OF OUR CLASS.
(BUT NOT EVERYONE HAS THE CAPACITY TO APPRECIATE MY WORK.)
FOR DRAWING. ALL THE TIME.
croquis
I LISTEN TO OLD BANDS. YOU PROBABLY HAVEN'T HEARD OF THEM.
OK FINE, I HAVE A SWEET TOOTH. BUT DON'T TELL ANYONE, PLS.
A BOOK THAT'S SUPER DARK AND DEEP.
Les fleurs du Mal

A FIFTEEN-FOOT-TALL STALK OF BROCCOLI!
TOMI HERE SAW HIS LIFE FLASH BEFORE HIS EYES.
ALL HOPE SEEMED LOST. WHEN SUDDENLY...
...WONDER PONY APPEARED! AN AMAZING HEROINE WITH UNBELIEVABLE STRENGTH!
OOOOOOOH!
WHAM! KICK! BAM! PUNCH!
THE MONSTER FELL TO THE FLOOR!
REDUCED TO MUSH BY THE STRENGTH OF WONDER PONY!
WOW, HE'S A GREAT STORY-TELLER!
YEAH...
THEN SHE RODE AGAIN INTO THE NIGHT, HER NOBLE STEED'S MANE FLYING IN THE WIND.
I SUPPOSE HE DOES HAVE A CERTAIN KNACK FOR NARRATIVE...
DOES HE REALLY EXPECT ANYONE TO BUY HIS ASININE STORIES?

BUT SAM WAS WRONG. ALL PEOPLE TALKED ABOUT THAT DAY AND THE NEXT WAS WONDER PONY.
A TWENTY-FOUR-FOOT MONSTER!
LOOK! I'VE GOT A PONYTAIL JUST LIKE HER!
I HAD ONE BEFORE WONDER PONY WAS A THING.
MY HAIR'S STILL TOO SHORT...
WE'RE TRAINING TWICE AS HARD NOW, SO WE CAN BE STRONG LIKE HER SOMEDAY!
HAVE A SEAT, CHILDREN.
I'VE GRADED YOUR ESSAYS. I'M QUITE DISAPPOINTED.
WOULD SOMEONE PLEASE REMIND ME OF THE TOPIC?
OUI, MONSIEUR!
YES, CAMILLE?
REWRITE THE LAST SCENE OF VICTOR HUGO'S NOVEL *THE LAST DAY OF A CONDEMNED MAN* IN THE THIRD PERSON.
THANK YOU.

AND NOW, CAN SOMEONE ENLIGHTEN ME AS TO WHAT HAPPENS IN THAT SCENE?
STEPHANIE?
THE NARRATOR IS LED TO HIS FATE, TO THE CHEERS OF THE CROWD.
VICTOR HUGO IS CONDEMNING THE SPECTACLE BEING MADE OF--
YES, YES. THANK YOU.
AND NOW, ADA, CAN YOU TELL ME WHERE YOU READ THAT THE PROTAGONIST WAS SAVED BY, I QUOTE, "A YOUNG PONY GIRL"?
THAT'LL BE A ZERO FOR YOU, YOUNG MISS.
WAIT!
THE BOOK ENDS BEFORE THE EXECUTION, SO MAYBE SUPER PONY *DID* SAVE HIM! HOW DO YOU KNOW?
UNFAIR! THAT GRADE IS UNFAIR!
IF SUPER PONY HAD BEEN THERE, SHE WOULD'VE SAVED HIM FOR SURE!
EXCEPT THERE'S NO SUCH THING AS SUPER PONY!
HOW CAN YOU SAY THAT? WHAT ABOUT TOMI?
WHATEVER!
HUGO
PSST! IT'S WONDER PONY!

THE ANTI-WONDER PONY CAMP HAD ALREADY SENT THREE KIDS TO THE NURSE WHEN THE VICE PRINCIPAL BURST IN.
BUT IN THE END, NO ONE GOT HURT BADLY.
THEN IT'S ALL OK!
NO, IT'S NOT!!
NOT A SINGLE ONE OF THEM GOT MY NAME RIGHT!
DO YOU EVEN REALIZE? IT'S NOT A HARD NAME! WONDER PONY!
HUH.
I'M NOT REALLY FEELING THE SYMPATHY.
WELL, I DON'T REALLY HAVE A NAME, SO HOW WOULD I UNDERSTAND?
WELL, WHY DON'T YOU PICK ONE?
WHAT WOULD YOU LIKED TO BE CALLED?
WHAT?
I CAN...PICK?
SERIOUSLY? JEAN-PIERRE?
CLASSY, RIGHT?
THAT'S ALWAYS BEEN MY FAVORITE NAME!

THERE YOU ARE!
TALKING TO YOUR TOY PONY?
N-NO! OF COURSE NOT!
HEY, IT'S JEAN-PIERRE FROM NOW ON, OK?
IT'S ALREADY CURFEW. WE NEVER GET TO GO OUT.
OR HAVE ANY FUN...
COME ON. IN YOUR ROOM. I CAN'T DEAL WITH YOU RIGHT NOW.
PLEASE! JUST FIVE MORE MINUTES!
IF YOU'RE BORED, DO YOUR HOMEWORK.
CLAC
PFF! THIS SCHOOL SUCKS!
KNOCK

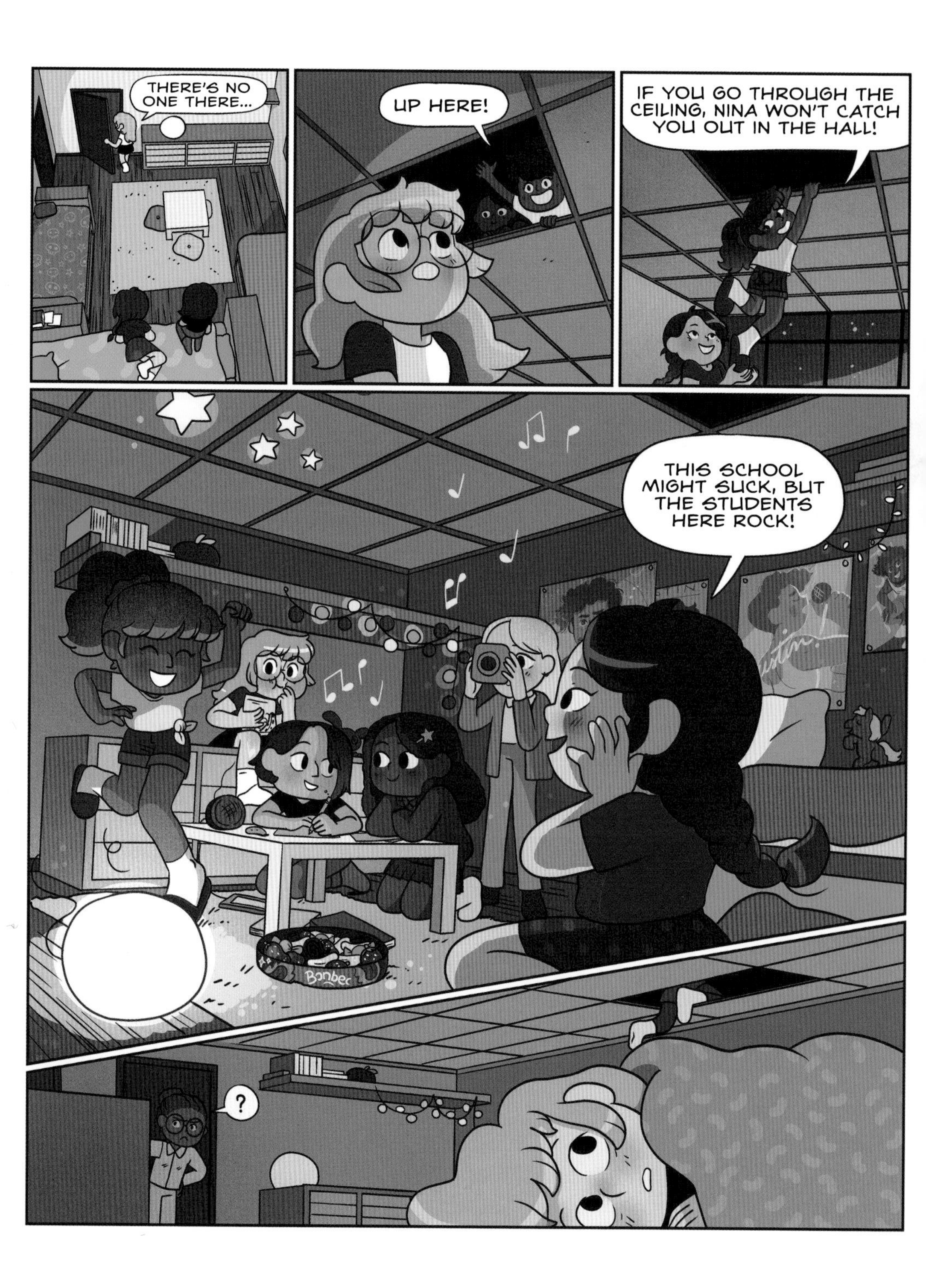
THERE'S NO ONE THERE...
UP HERE!
IF YOU GO THROUGH THE CEILING, NINA WON'T CATCH YOU OUT IN THE HALL!
THIS SCHOOL MIGHT SUCK, BUT THE STUDENTS HERE ROCK!
Bonbec
?

MANI
YOUR DELEGATE
HI, EVERYBODY!
IT WAS A TOUGH CAMPAIGN, BUT I WON!
I'VE GOT TONS OF IDEAS TO MAKE OUR LIFE HERE GREAT!
CURFEW IS AN UNFAIR RESTRICTION ON OUR FREEDOM. I'M THROWING SECRET PARTIES TO PROTEST.
WHAT DO WE WANT? FRIES! AT! LUNCH!
SUSTENANCE DURING STRIKES.
Cookycroc

elect your REPRESENTATIVES
VOTE MANI
MANI
VOTE FOR GAIL
VOTE MANI
OK?
GAIL
for delegate
VOTE. MANI
GAIL
GAIL!
AGENDA

NOW CAN YOU TELL ME WHY WE ABSOLUTELY **HAD** TO GET UP ON THE ROOF AT MIDNIGHT?
IT'S ONE OF YOUR DUTIES.
PATROLLING EVERY NOW AND THEN TO MAKE SURE NO MONSTERS ARE LURKING NEARBY.
OH. ARE ANY?
WE'RE GOOD. WE CAN GO BACK TO BED NOW.
HURRY IT UP, WILL YA? I'M BEAT.

?
POF
ALEXIS WANTS TO HANG OUT AFTER CLASS. WILL YOU COME WITH ME?
OH, I DUNNO...I DON'T KNOW HIM. BESIDES, HE WANTS YOU.
MAX, QUEL ÂGE AS-TU?
UH...COMME ÇI, COMME ÇA?
PSST! I THINK THEY'RE FRIENDS! MAYBE MAX'LL BE THERE TOO! YOUR...

...LOVERBOY!
OK, OK! I HAVE NO IDEA WHAT YOU'RE TALKING ABOUT, BUT I'LL COME WITH!
À DEMAIN!
VIVE WONDE PON
I CAN'T STAND THIS PONY GIRL STUFF!
PONIES ARE THE WIMPIEST ANIMAL.
WELL, MAYBE SHE HAD NO CHOICE.
HEY, SAM! LOUISON!
SAM, EVERYONE KNOWS YOU'RE AN AMAAAZING ARTIST! WE NEED YOUR HELP...
...TO DESIGN A LOGO FOR OUR WONDER PONY FAN CLUB!

OOH, A FAN CLUB! WHAT A GREAT IDEA!
WILL YOU HELP US, SAM?
UH...SURE!
OH! IT'S OUR TREASURER!
WOW! HE'S A WONDER PONY FAN, TOO?
MAX, SAM AGREED TO DRAW US A MASCOT! IT'LL BE AWESOME!
COOL!
HERE, I MADE A SKETCH. IF YOU LIKE IT, I CAN INK IT.
WAY COOL! SHE LOOKS AWESOME! I LOVE HER FACE!
COOL!
I COULD DRAW HER THROWING A PUNCH. MIGHT BE MORE DYNAMIC!
GOOD IDEA! YOU CAN DO THAT?
OH, IT'S NOT HARD...
HMPH! THAT'S NOT WHAT SHE LOOKS LIKE AT ALL!

THAT DOESN'T REALLY MATTER. WE JUST WANT A COOL LOGO.
HOW WOULD YOU KNOW? YOU'VE NEVER SEEN HER!
YEAH. NO ONE *ACTUALLY* KNOWS WHAT SHE LOOKS LIKE.
YEAH.
NUH-UH! I KNOW EXACTLY WHAT SHE LOOKS LIKE. I SAW HER IN THE HALLWAY ONCE, AND SHE EVEN SAID HI TO ME.
WE'RE PRACTICALLY FRIENDS.
WHAT?
UH... ALMOST. ALMOST.
I COULD EVEN GET YOU HER AUTOGRAPH, IF YOU WANT.
AS IF!
WHAT? YOU WANT ONE TOO?
QUIT SPOUTING NONSENSE! THERE'S NO WAY YOU KNOW HER!
OH, DON'T BE JEALOUS! EVERYONE HAS THEIR OWN THING. YOU DRAW, AND I'M WONDER PONY'S BESTIE.

YOU'RE SUCH A HUGE LIAR! YOUR SO-CALLED PONY GIRL ISN'T EVEN REAL!
YES, SHE IS, AND HER NAME IS ***WONDER PONY!***
OH, YEAH? THEN PROVE IT! NEXT TIME BRING A PHOTO!
I WILL!
FINE, THEN!
NO PROBLEM!
WHY WOULD LOUISON LIE?
CAN'T YOU TELL SHE'S JUST TRYING TO IMPRESS--
IMPRESS WHO?
NO ONE. DROP IT.
HAH! YOU ADMIT I'M RIGHT!
WHATEVER. BYE, LOUISON.

NINA
YEAH?
I JUST LOVE MATH! BUT I HAVE TO BE AN RESIDENT ASSISTANT TO PAY MY WAY THROUGH SCHOOL...
...AND, OBVIOUSLY, THE KIDS SPEND ALL THEIR TIME KEEPING ME FROM STUDYING.
"YADDA YADDA HELP ME NINA! IT HURTS!"
"YADDA YADDA NINA, I SAW A MONSTER!"
WHO HAS TIME FOR ALL THAT?!

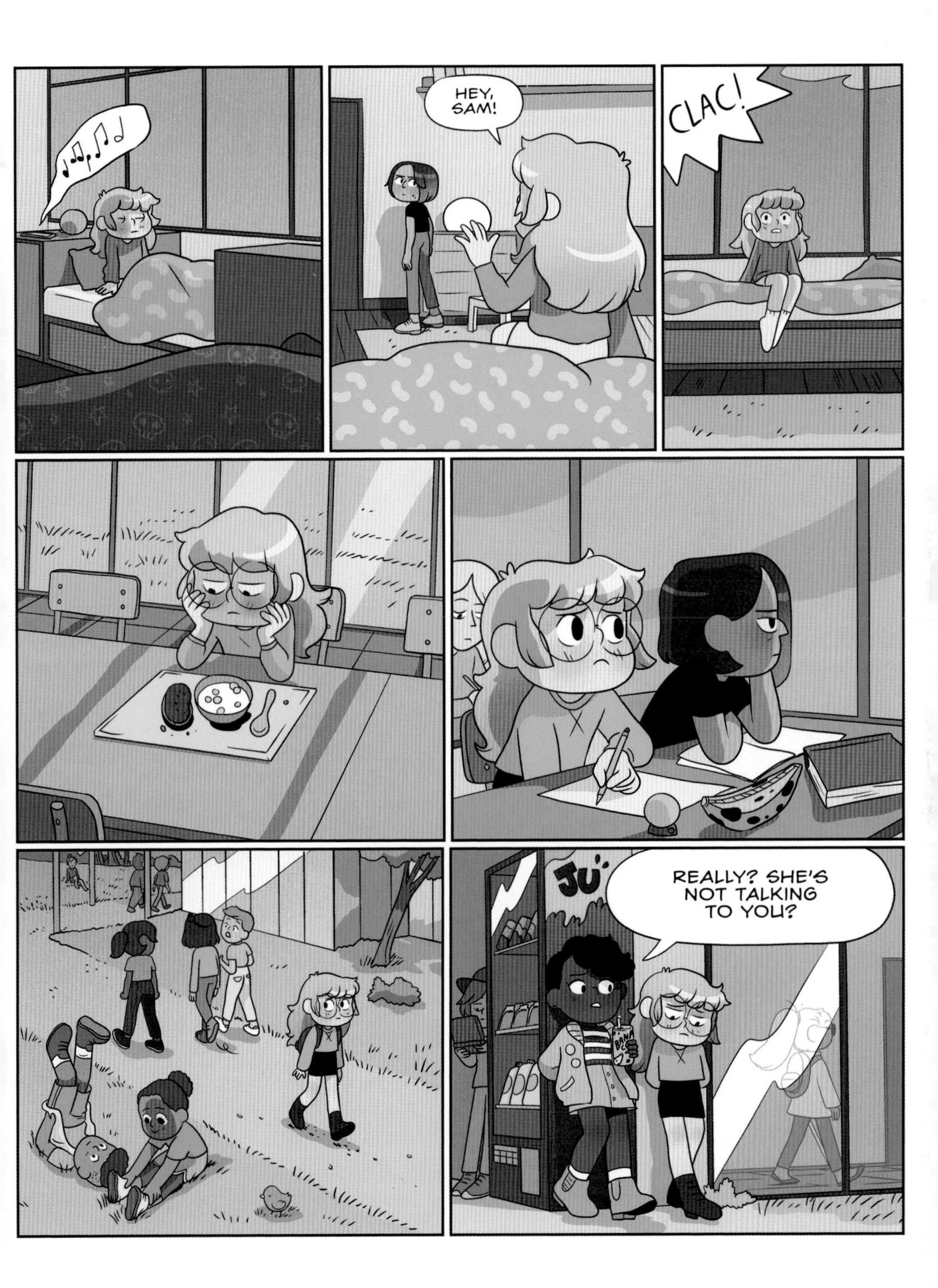
HEY, SAM!
CLAC!
JU
REALLY? SHE'S NOT TALKING TO YOU?

WE HAD A LITTLE FIGHT.
OH, YEAH? WHAT HAPPENED?
SOME KIDS ASKED HER TO DRAW WONDER PONY, AND SHE MESSED IT ALL UP.
I OUGHTA KNOW. I'VE SEEN WONDER PONY.
SO I TOLD HER, AND INSTEAD OF THANKING ME AND FIXING HER DRAWING, SHE GOT MAD.
WHATEVER!
AND NOW SHE WON'T TALK TO ME, AND EVERYONE THINKS I'M A LIAR.
I HATE HER!
Y'KNOW, A REAL FRIEND KNOWS WHEN YOU'RE LYING. AND DOESN'T TRY TO STEAL YOUR THUNDER.
THAT'S IT! I NEVER REALIZED HOW MEAN SHE WAS BEING!
UH...

TU
THANKS A TON, CHARLIE!
I DON'T KNOW IF YOU--
SHE'LL SEE WHO THE LIAR IS!
--REALLY GOT WHAT I WAS TRYING TO SAY.
JEAN-PIERRE! I HAVE AN IDEA!
TURN ME INTO WONDER PONY. WE'LL TAKE A PHOTO, AND SHOW EVERYONE. SAM WILL SEE I WAS RIGHT, AND NO ONE WILL CALL ME A LIAR, AND I'LL BE SUPER POPULAR!
NO.
WHADDAYA MEAN, NO? IT'S A GREAT IDEA! C'MON, DO IT!
NO. JUST KEEP YOUR MOUTH SHUT NEXT TIME.
PLEASE, PLEASE, PLEASE!
POWERS ARE SERIOUS THINGS! YOU DON'T JUST USE THEM TO SHOW OFF!
AHHH! HELP! A MOOONSTER!
HEEEELP!
YES!

OK, HOW ARE WE GONNA DO THIS...
...AND GET A GOOD SHOT?
COUNT ME OUT.
NO PROBLEM.
EVER SEEN A SELFIE STICK, YOU GROUCHY OLD PONY?
AAAAH
OK, ENOUGH FOR NOW. LET'S GO!
HMF!

WHERE WERE YOU?
HEY! COME BACK HERE!
COME BACK AND FIGHT, YOU SPIDER!
I BELIEVE WE'RE A BIT LATE...

I, UH...SCARED HIM OFF! WE'RE GOOD! HE WON'T BE BACK!
WHAT A MESS. GAIL! KIM! GET INSIDE.
AND HELP TOMI TO THE NURSE! HE'S BLEEDING ALL OVER THE PLACE.
MA'AM, DIDN'T YOU SEE THE GIANT MONSTER?
YOU'D BETTER GO WITH TOMI AND GET YOUR HEAD CHECKED, MANI.

GAZE LOST IN THE DISTANCE...
I TEACH FRENCH AT THIS MISERABLE SCHOOL.
I ADORE GREAT LITERATURE. A PITY I MUST SHARE IT WITH THESE IGNORANT URCHINS.
I'D ALREADY PENNED MY FIRST POEMS BY AGE 5.
DARE I SAY I'M A GENIUS?
I DARE!
MY PASSION? WRITING EARTH-SHATTERING LOVE LETTERS.
(I'VE NO ONE TO SEND THEM TO FOR NOW, SO IN THE MEANTIME, I ADDRESS THEM TO MYSELF.)
Mon amour,
Je ne peux ni
BALLPOINT IS SO CRUDE.

YOU CAN'T STAY IN THIS CABINET FOREVER!
WHY BOTHER GOING OUT? I'M THE MOST USELESS SUPER-HEROINE EVER...
HEY, JEAN-PIERRE? WHERE ARE ALL THESE MONSTERS COMING FROM?
I'VE BEEN LOOKING INTO THAT FOR A WHILE. IT'S NOT CLEAR TO ME YET.
BUT I HAVE A THEORY: WHEN SOMETHING REALLY, REALLY SCARES A STUDENT, THEIR FEAR MATERIALIZES AS A MONSTER THAT SOWS CHAOS ALL OVER THE SCHOOL.

THE GIANT SPIDER, FOR INSTANCE: THAT'S A CLASSIC. LOTS OF PEOPLE ARE AFRAID OF SPIDERS.
THOUGH OFTEN THE CREATURE THAT APPEARS IS A THOUSAND TIMES FREAKIER THAN A SPIDER.
BUT BEWARE! IT CAN BE A LOT MORE COMPLICATED THAN THAT!
UH-OH! QUICK, GET UP!
I THOUGHT YOU WERE SO ASHAMED YOU WERE GOING TO HIDE FOREVER?
WELL, I MIGHT'VE SAID THAT...
...BUT RIGHT NOW, IT'S SELFIE TIME!

SAM! SAM!
THERE YOU ARE!
SEE? SHE'S REAL! YOU GOTTA BELIEVE ME NOW.
WHAT'S YOUR DAMAGE? I DON'T CARE ABOUT YOUR WONDER PONY!
REALLY? BUT LAST TIME YOU GOT MAD WHEN I SAID I KNEW HER?
DO YOU NOT CARE ANYMORE, 'CAUSE SHE KINDA MESSED UP ON HER LAST FIGHT?
NO! I'M MAD BECAUSE OF WHAT YOU DID TO ME, NOT BECAUSE YOU BELIEVE IN PONY SUPERHEROINES!
FORGET IT.

IS YOUR GOTH FRIEND MAD AT YOU?
UH...SHE'S NOT REALLY A GOTH.
HMPH! I DON'T GET HER. SHE'S ALWAYS MAD ABOUT SOMETHING!
SHE GOES FOR A GOTH LOOK, BUT SHE DOESN'T HAVE TRUE GOTH SPIRIT, SEE?
UH-HUH...
HEY, WAIT--YOU LIKE BROCCOLI?
I DON'T REALLY HAVE A CHOICE.

I HAVE A DISEASE. I HAVE TO EAT MEGA HEALTHY. NEVER TOO MUCH FAT OR SUGAR. I HAVE TO BE CAREFUL, OR I COULD GET REALLY SICK.
IF HE HAS CANDY, HE'S DEAD!
NO, YOU BUTTHEAD--
BUT TOMI, YOU DON'T HAVE TO WORRY TOO MUCH, RIGHT? YOU GET SPECIAL MEALS MADE FOR YOU HERE.
SHOULDN'T YOU BE MORE SCARED OF CAKE THAN BROCCOLI?
HUH?
HELLO, DAD?
YEAH. I GOT BROCCOLI, LENTILS, AND AN APPLE FOR DESSERT.
HIS DAD CALLS HIM AT EVERY MEAL TO MAKE SURE.
OK, I WON'T EAT THE WHOLE APPLE. PROMISE. BYE, DAD.

THAT'S WHAT I MEANT WHEN I SAID IT WAS MORE COMPLICATED.
IT'S NOT THAT TOMI HATES BROCCOLI, OR EVEN THAT HE'S SCARED OF HAVING TOO MUCH SUGAR.
WHAT FRIGHTENS HIM IS WHEN HIS FATHER CALLS HIM JUST TO ASK WHAT HE'S EATING.
OH.
SIGH...THIS *IS* MORE COMPLICATED THAN I THOUGHT.
YOU DON'T HAVE TO THINK TOO HARD. ALL ***YOU*** HAVE TO DO IS FIGHT MONSTERS.

HMPH! APPARENTLY, SOME TOY PONY IS MORE INTERESTING THAN SPENDING TIME WITH ME!
WHO CARES! I CAN MAKE OTHER FRIENDS!
HMPH! I'M FINE ON MY OWN.
ZOUIP!
HUH?
ZOUIP ?
YOU'RE PRETTY FIERCE FOR A LITTLE SQUIRREL!
HEY, SAM!

WANNA PARTNER UP FOR THE FRENCH PRESENTATION? I MEAN, ONLY IF YOU WANNA...
OH! UH...
IF YOU DON'T WANT TO STUDY, WE COULD READ SOME MANGA...
I LIKE READING, AND YOU LIKE DRAWING...
MANGA'S SOMETHING BOTH OF US SHOULD LIKE.
YOU COULD SAY SOMETHING, INSTEAD OF JUST MAKING WEIRD FACES.
OH, WELL...NEVER MIND.

HEY! WHAT'S YOUR PROBLEM?!
YOU CAN'T JUST DO SOMETHING LIKE THAT, EVEN IF YOU ARE CUTE!
HEY, SAM...
...WE STILL REALLY DIG THAT DRAWING, BUT WE'RE KIND OF OVER WONDER PONY, SINCE SHE STOPPED SAVING PEOPLE.
WE WERE THINKING WE'D DO A SCHOOL PAPER, AND...
OH! WHO'S THIS?
HE'S SOME KIND OF SQUIRREL, BUT HE'S KIND OF--
GNAP
HEY! GET A HOLD OF YOUR PET!
BUT HE'S NOT MINE! I--
IT'S OK, LET'S JUST GO. NO NEED TO GET ANGRY.
WHAT DO YOU WANT, ANYWAY? LEAVE ME ALONE NOW!
CLAC

WAIT! I'M SO SORRY!
ZWEEP! ZWEEP!
IT'S NOT A BIG DEAL. I JUST DON'T LOVE YOUR PET, SAM. SEE YOU LATER?
YOU HAVE A SQUIRREL? YOU BETTER HIDE IT. IF NINA SEES YOU--
STAY BACK!
WHOA! I'M JUST TRYING TO HELP!
GO AHEAD! BE ALL ALONE!
NO, IT'S JUST THAT...
HE'S DANGEROUS!

ALEXIS
HI, EVERY-BODY!
I'M THE EDITOR-IN-CHIEF OF THE SCHOOL PAPER!
THESE DAYS, WONDER PONY'S ON EVERYONE'S LIPS--TOO MUCH SO, SAY DETRACTORS. BUT IT'S SUCH AN EXCITING TOPIC!
JOURNAL
NOTES
AN AUDIO RECORDER FOR INTERVIEWS!
MY DREAM? A WONDER PONY INTERVIEW IN MY PAPER!

I THOUGHT I HEARD A MONSTER IN THE FRIDGE...

SHE EVEN ADOPTED A SQUIRREL SO SHE WON'T HAVE TO TALK TO ME ANYMORE!
ISN'T THAT SQUIRREL OF HERS KIND OF SCARY?
LET ME GO PLAY WITH EVERYONE ELSE! I'M SICK OF YOU!
I DON'T KNOW...
RIGHT FROM THE START SHE WAS ALWAYS SAYING SHE WAS JUST FINE ON HER OWN.
MAYBE SHE'S JUST AS SAD AS YOU ARE ABOUT NOT BEING FRIENDS.

HAH! I USED TO SAY THAT TOO, WHEN I FIRST GOT HERE!
YOU?
YEAH, I USED TO TELL EVERYONE: "I'M NOT HERE TO MAKE FRIENDS!"
BUT YOU'RE THE NICEST, FRIENDLIEST PERSON IN THE WHOLE SCHOOL!
HMM...THAT MUST BE WHY I CAN NEVER DRINK MY SODA IN PEACE...
WAS IT TRUE? DID YOU REALLY NOT WANT FRIENDS?
OF COURSE NOT!
THEN WHY'D YOU SAY THAT?
GUESS!

SHE MAKES A GOOD POINT.
AND THAT SQUIRREL'S GROWING PRETTY FAST!
WHAT ARE YOU TRYING TO SAY?
YOU THINK IT'S...
UH-OH.
A MONSTER!

TOO BAD SAM'S NOT MY FRIEND ANYMORE. I COULD'VE SAVED HER.
NOOO! SAM!

WHATDOIDO?! WHATDOIDO?!
C'MON! THE WORLD NEEDS WONDER PONY RIGHT NOW, MORE THAN EVER!
BUT--
DON'T WORRY. I'LL HELP YOU.
POUF
HURRY! THEY'RE ON THE ROOF!
DON'T TAKE THE STAIRS! USE YOUR SUPER-MUSCLES!
YOU CAN LEAP UP THERE!

WOW!
YOU WERE RIGHT, JEAN-PIERRE! THIS TIME, I'M GOING TO FIGHT FOR REAL! I'M NOT SCARED ANYMORE!

YOU CAN DO IT!
UPPERCUT! LEFT HOOK, RIGHT HOOK!
BACK KICK!
AND FLYING SPINNING KICK! BAM!

OVER HERE, FUZZY!
UPPERCUT! LEFT HOOK, RIGHT HOOK!
BAM
BACK KICK!
PAF
FLYING... SPINNING...

...KICK!
BAM

SHBAM
HEY! I DID WHAT I WAS SUPPOSED TO!
JEAN-PIERRE, WHY'S IT STILL MOVING?
IMPROVISE!

WONDER PONY! IS THAT YOU?
DUH!!
YOU CAME TO SAVE ME?
SO YOU BELIEVE I'M REAL NOW?
WHY WOULD YOU CARE ABOUT ME? EVERYONE ELSE HATES ME.
WHAT ARE YOU TALKING ABOUT? YOU ALWAYS SAID YOU DIDN'T NEED FRIENDS!
YEAH, WELL... MAYBE I WASN'T TELLING THE WHOLE TRUTH THEN.
WAIT, SO *THAT'S* YOUR FEAR?
BEING ALONE?
BUT I THOUGHT YOU--

STOP TRYING TO UNDERSTAND. ALL I HAVE TO DO IS FIGHT MONSTERS.
HMM...

AAHH
BUT THAT PRETTY BLONDE IN YOUR CLASS IS YOUR FRIEND, RIGHT? LOUISON?
I DUNNO...
WHAT DO YOU MEAN, YOU DUNNO?
I'M SURE SHE IS. SHE TOLD ME SO.
'CAUSE WE KNOW EACH OTHER.
REALLY? LOUISON SAID WE WERE STILL FRIENDS?
ZOUiiiP !
PSHHT

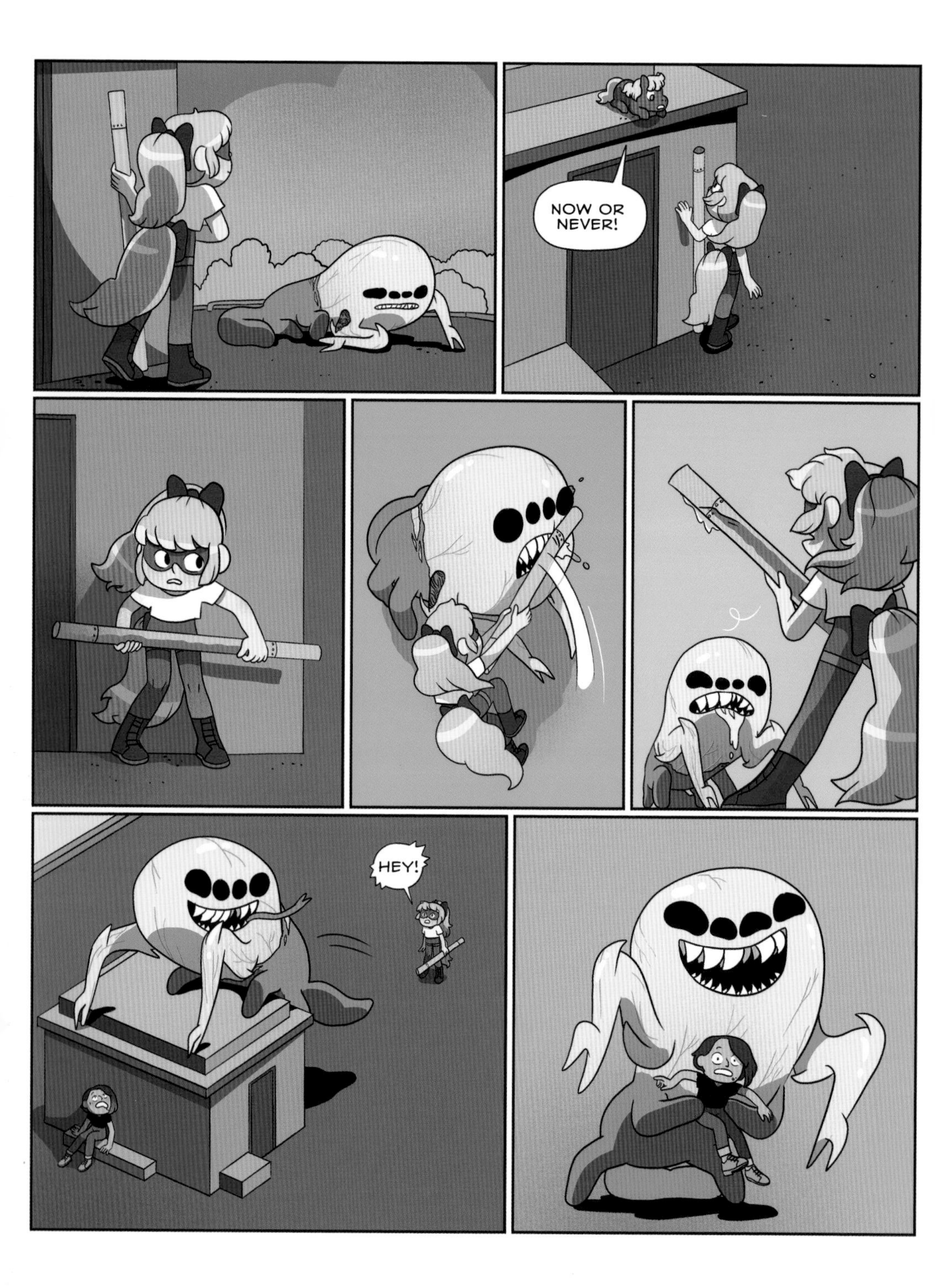
NOW OR NEVER!
HEY!

NUH-UH!!
SHAM

WOW...
NO NEED FOR THANKS. JUST DOING MY JOB!
UH...SO, I WAS WONDERING. IF LOUISON'S REALLY MY FRIEND, WHY'D SHE ACT LIKE THAT THE OTHER DAY?
HUH?
MY WORK HERE IS DONE! GOTTA RUN!
'BYE!

TOMI
EEEK!
AAAAAH!
OUCH
SOMETIMES, I FEEL LIKE I'M JINXED.
SO I COLLECT LUCKY CHARMS!
Delichou
0% SUGAR • 100% DELICIOUS
A GIFT FROM DAD
(GROSS)
GOOD THING THE COOK SAVES ME SNACKS TO NIBBLE ON!
YUM! RAW CARROTS!
(I WON'T LIE. IT DOESN'T SEEM TO WORK VERY WELL...)

PRINCIPAL
TOC TOC TOC
AH, THERE YOU ARE, PONY.
OUR NEW RECRUIT'S LEARNING THE ROPES.
I SAW HER ACCOMPLISHMENTS ON THE ROOFTOP.
YOU'RE AS GOOD A TEACHER AS EVER.
LET'S HOPE SHE SURVIVES HER YEARS HERE...

UH...CAN I HAVE A LITTLE CHAT WITH YOU?
JUSTIN
IT TOOK ME A WHILE, BUT I THINK I FINALLY FIGURED OUT WHY YOU WERE MAD AT ME.
IT WAS BECAUSE I ACTED LIKE A BIG JERK.
A BIG JEALOUS JERK, EVEN. YOUR DRAWING WAS GREAT, BUT I WANTED THEM TO PAY ATTENTION TO ME.
"THEM"? WHO'S "THEM"?
HUH? OH, UH...NO ONE SPECIAL!

BUT THAT'S NOT HOW FRIENDS BEHAVE.
ESPECIALLY NOT BEST FRIENDS.
WELL, IN THE END YOU WERE RIGHT. WONDER PONY'S REAL.
GOOD THING SHE SHOWED UP, TOO.
I GUESS SHE'S PRETTY COOL...
SAY, SINCE YOU KNOW HER, COULD YOU GIVE HER THIS?

IT'S A LOGO. SUITS HER TO A TEE, RIGHT?
WONDER PONY
SHE'LL LOVE IT!
WANNA COME OVER TO MY HOUSE OVER BREAK?
WE'LL BAKE CAKES AND WEAR HALLOWEEN COSTUMES!
WHOA. THAT'S SO GIRLY...
I'LL CHECK MY SCHEDULE AND SEE IF I CAN FIT YOU IN.

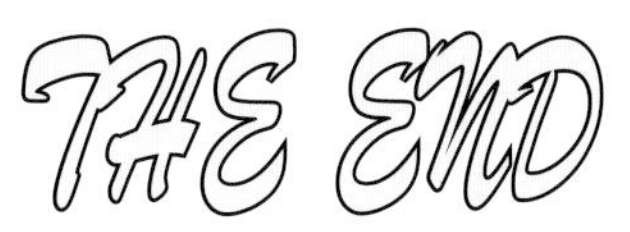
THE END

MANI
KIM
STEPHANIE
CAMILLE
ANIS
NOËLLE
GAIL
ANN
ALEXIS
ADA
TOMI
LOUISON
SAM
ERIN

chomp
chomp

WONDER PONY™

TEACHING GUIDE

Learning Standards

The questions and activities in this teacher Guide correlate with the following Common Core English Language Arts Standards (www.corestandards.org) for Grades 4-8:

ELA Reading: Literature Standards

- Key Ideas and Details RL.4-8.1, RL.4-8.2, RL.4-8.3;
- Craft and Structure RL.4-8.4, RL.4-8.5, RL.4-8.6.

ELA Reading: Informational Texts Standards

- Key Ideas and Details RI.4-8.1, RI.4-8.2, RI.4-8.3;
- Craft and Structure RI.4-8.4, RI.4-8.5;
- Integration of Knowledge and Ideas RI.4-8.7, RI.4-8.8.

ELA Writing Standards

- Text Types and Purposes W.4-8.1, W.4-8.3;
- Production and Distribution of Writing W.4-8.4, W.4-8.5;
- Research to Build and Present Knowledge W.4-8.8, W.4-8.9.

ELA Speaking and Listening Standards

- Comprehension and Collaboration SL.4-8.1;
- Presentation of Knowledge and Ideas SL.4-8.4, SL.4-8.5.

A General Approach

It is highly recommended that you read Scott McCloud's *Understanding Comics*[1], specifically pages 60-63, which deal with closure, pages 70-72, which deal with panel transitions and 152-155, which deal with word/picture combinations. Depending on the needs of your class, you can have students learn these specific terms and use them to identify the different transition and combination styles. Alternately, you can utilize your understanding of them to guide discussion, when examining specific panels or pages.

Highlight individual panels and or pages, and ask the following questions:

- What is going on in this panel or on this page?
- What is the purpose of the specific pictures in telling the story? How do they enhance the words?
- Why did the creator choose to put these words and pictures together in this way?
- How does color affect the scene?
- What do we learn about the character from the images?
- What mood is being set and how?

Examine the specific sequence of panels:

- Why did the creator put these panels in this particular order?
- What's happening between the panels?
- How does the transition between these panels indicate things like mood and character?
- How do the panel transitions affect the speed of the scene?
- Why did the creator choose this speed?

Let's get active!
A great exercise is to have students act out a short scene in the book, getting them to fill in the action occurring between the panels. This demonstrates to them that the gutter (that space between panels) is just as important as the other storytelling elements in the book.

1. McCloud, Scott, 1960-. *Understanding Comics : the Invisible Art*. New York :HarperPerennial, 1994.

Discussion Questions

Questions about specific pages:

1. Discuss the bottom panel of page 12. Describe the layout of this panel. What does information does this layout help to convey?

2. Examine the backgrounds of panels 2 and 3 on page 13. What do they add to the narrative?
3. What do you learn about the three roommates from the scene on page 16?
4. On page 19, Louison says "She kind of flaunts it, doesn't she?" about Charlie. What does she mean by that?
5. What is going on on page 20, panel 4?
6. On page 31, the first 4 panels have a slightly different color palette and texture. What is the difference between those panels and the others on that page? Why does the change happen?
7. On page 37, why does Louison take credit for defeating the broccoli monster? Why does Tomi believe her?

8. On page 42, all the kids are going Wonder Pony crazy. Have you ever changed yourself to emulate someone famous? Why or why not?
9. Discuss the first panel on page 54. Why is it constructed the way it is? Examine layout, background, and color.
10. What emotions are shown on page 67? What are the visual elements that show the characters' emotions?

11. On page 92, why does Louison leave instead of answering Sam's question?

12. Page 95 reveals some interesting information. What elements are included in this page to make it more spooky? What does this page do to you as a reader? What do you think will happen to Louison?

13. Discuss the final page of the book. Why do you think this particular layout was chosen? Do you think it makes an effective ending?

General Questions:

1. Based on the monsters that appear in the book (broccoli, spider, squirrel), what are the characteristics of a monster?

2. The monsters appear as manifestations of student fear. In mythology, there are many monsters that exist because of a cultural fear. Discuss mythological monster stories and the fears those different monsters represent.

3. What causes Louison to believe in her ability to fight the monsters? Does this happen slowly or quickly? Can you find moments in the book that lead up to her being able to truly be Wonder Pony?

BONUS QUESTION: Discuss what it means to be a superhero.

- What are the characteristics of a superhero?
- Are there any problems at your school that a superhero could help with?
- Are there any ways that you could be a superhero yourself?

4. How does Wonder Pony affect Louison's friendship with Sam?

5. Louison consistently feels it necessary to respond to the rumors about Wonder Pony. Why does she do this? Do you think it's a good idea? When is it a good idea to defend the truth and when it is not?

6. How do Louison and Sam repair their friendship? Why do you think they make such good friends?

Activities

Reading

2.

1. Based on all the adventures throughout the book, make a map of the school and identify the locations where the different fights happen between Wonder Pony and the fear monsters.

2. Discuss one or more of the character pages on pages 15, 29, 32, etc. Do they show the whole story about those characters? How much of the character sheets are how the characters want to be seen? What are some of the inner traits of each character that you could add to their character sheets? Create an inner traits character sheet for one character and compare it to the outward trait character sheet in the book.

3. Many panels have only a simple pattern or a single color as their background. What is the purpose of these panels? Pick three of these panels, choosing ones with distinct colors or patterns, and explain how the background effects the mood, characters, or story in those panels.

Writing

1. Write a short story, either in prose or comic form that includes one of the scenes shown in the chapter breaks on pages 30, 40, 56, 64,76.

1.

2. On page 67, Jean-Pierre explains that the monsters are a manifestation of the students' fears. What are you afraid of? Design your own monster. Create an artist statement explaining your choice.

3. Create your own character sheet (like the ones on pages 15, 29, 32, etc.) showing your outward traits. You can draw or use photos. Write a reflection about how you think other people see you. Is that how you want to be seen? What traits do you think people don't see? Do you wish they would see those things? Why would you want to hide some traits?

4. Examine the choices Louison makes on page 60. Have you ever made a selfish decision that you regret? Write a letter to someone you may have hurt through your decisions.

5. Write a diary entry from either Jean-Pierre's point of view on getting to choose his own name (page 44), or Sam's point of view about the events on pages 57 to 64.

Speaking

1. *"A real friend knows when you're lying. And doesn't try to steal your thunder."*, p58.

   Discuss this in groups of three. What does this mean? What do you think a real friend is? How do your ideas compare to those of the others in your group? Create a Venn diagram that shows the overlap of your group's ideas of friendship.

2. In groups, decide on a problem that you would like to solve in your school community. Create your own superhero that will work as a team with the other heroes in your group to fight that problem. Make sure each hero has a superhero name, powers, and a costume. Present your team and the problem you'd fight against to your class.

Party Time! Optional: Have a superhero party, in which each student dresses up as the hero they created.

3. In groups, create and record a school news broadcast, about the school election, or about one of the fights between Wonder Pony and a monster.

Integrating

1. Monsters exist in a variety of mythological stories in many cultures. Identify and research a mythological monster in a culture that is not your own. Describe the fear that that monster represents and how the story alleviates that fear.

2. Look at the election posters on page 48 and examine the election posters in your area. What makes a good election poster? Design your own election poster.

3. Rewrite page 46 or 57 as a prose story. How is the story effected when the pictures are not there?

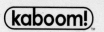